CONTENTS

William Shakespeare:

The Man, the Actor, the Author

William Shakespeare is considered to be one of the greatest writers who ever lived.

He was born in the market town of Stratford-upon-Avon in Warwickshire, England in 1564 and died there in 1616.

— SHAKESPEARE'S —

MUCH ADO
ABOUT NOTHING

Adapted by
Steve Barlow and Steve Skidmore

Illustrated by Wendy Tan Shiau Wei

W

FRANKLIN WATTS

LONDON • SYDNEY

FRANKLIN WATTS
FIRST PUBLISHED IN GREAT BRITAIN IN 2022
BY HODDER AND STOUGHTON

CREDITS:
EDITOR: GRACE GLENDINNING
DESIGNER: CATHRYN GILBERT
ILLUSTRATIONS: WENDY TAN SHIAU WEI

PICTURE CREDITS: PAGE 109 COLIN WATERS / ALAMY STOCK PHOTO
EVERY ATTEMPT HAS BEEN MADE TO CLEAR COPYRIGHT. SHOULD
THERE BE ANY INADVERTENT OMISSION PLEASE APPLY TO THE
PUBLISHER FOR RECTIFICATION.

HB ISBN: 978 1 4451 8010 6
PB ISBN: 978 1 4451 8011 3

PRINTED IN CHINA

FRANKLIN WATTS
AN IMPRINT OF
HACHETTE CHILDREN'S GROUP
PART OF HODDER AND STOUGHTON
CARMELITE HOUSE
50 VICTORIA EMBANKMENT
LONDON EC4Y ODZ

AN HACHETTE UK COMPANY
WWW.HACHETTE.CO.UK
WWW.HACHETTECHILDRENS.CO.UK

Shakespeare is usually referred to as an Elizabethan playwright but he actually lived during the reign of two monarchs: Elizabeth I and James I. When Elizabeth died in 1603, James, who was already King of Scotland, took over the English throne.

During Shakespeare's lifetime, he wrote nearly 40 plays and over 150 poems (mainly sonnets). He was also an actor, a very successful businessman and owned valuable buildings and land in London and Stratford.

His parents were John Shakespeare, a glove-maker and Stratford council official, and Mary Arden, who was the daughter of a wealthy local farmer. As the child of a reasonably well-off family, William attended the local grammar school, where he would have studied Latin and Greek as well as English literature and history.

In 1582, at the age of 18, he married Anne Hathaway. They had three children but by 1587, Shakespeare had left his wife and children in Stratford and moved to London. He joined an acting company and, by the early 1590s, was writing his own plays, becoming well known and successful in the world of London theatre.

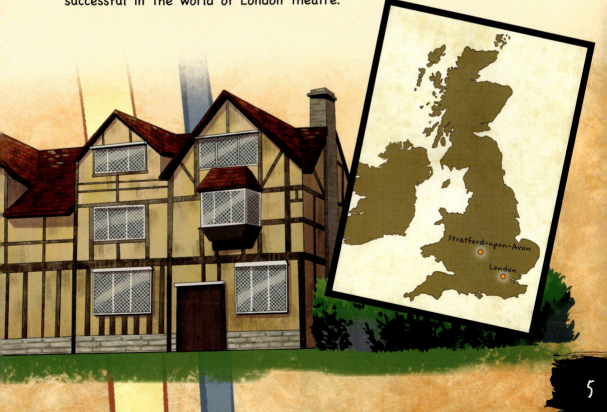

Stratford-upon-Avon

London

In 1594, Shakespeare joined a new acting company, The Lord Chamberlain's Men, with his friend, the actor Richard Burbage. He would spend the rest of his life writing plays to be performed by this company and even became a part-owner of The Globe Theatre, which was built in 1599. The Lord Chamberlain's Men were so successful that when King James came to the throne, he became their sponsor and their name was changed to The King's Men.

From 1610, Shakespeare began to spend more time in Stratford. He died on 23rd April 1616. In the years following Shakespeare's death, two of his friends, John Heminge and Henry Condell, collected manuscripts and copies of his plays. They were printed in 1623 in an edition known as *The First Folio*. This collection of tragedies, comedies and historical plays helped to establish Shakespeare as a great playwright – possibly the greatest the world has ever known.

Another friend, the playwright Ben Jonson, said that Shakespeare's plays would prove to be "not of an age, but for all time".

Jonson was right. Shakespeare's plays have been translated into every major language and are performed across the world. They have also been turned into films, TV series, musicals, ballets and graphic novels!

Much Ado About Nothing
– The Play

Shakespeare wrote plays of many different types. Among some of his greatest hits, *Hamlet* is a thriller, *A Midsummer Night's Dream* is a madcap comedy, *Romeo and Juliet* is a love story, *The Tempest* is a fantasy, *Macbeth* is a horror story — and *Much Ado About Nothing* is a rom-com.

It deals with two love affairs: one between Beatrice and Benedick, which begins with feuding, but ends quite differently; and one between Claudio and Hero that begins with sweetness and light, but nearly ends in disaster.

Much Ado About Nothing is believed to have been written in 1598, during the reign of Queen Elizabeth I. It appears in print in the *First Quarto* of 1600. It is likely that there were performances both before and after this date, though the first performance recorded seems to have been at the court of Elizabeth's successor King James I, in 1613.

The play is cleverly plotted with events coming thick and fast, and lots of verbal fireworks from memorable characters including the villainous Don John, warring lovers Beatrice and Benedick and the pompous Dogberry, Constable of the Watch.

It also has many memorable lines.

"I wonder that you are still talking, Signor Benedick. Nobody marks you."
Beatrice Act 1 Scene 1

"... There was a star danced, and under that I was born."
Beatrice Act 2 Scene 1

"Sigh no more, ladies, sigh no more. Men were deceivers ever ..."
Balthazar Act 2 Scene 3

"The world must be peopled."
Benedick Act 2 Scene 3

"For there was never yet philosopher That could endure the toothache patiently ..."
Leonato Act 5 Scene 1

The play is about love and marriage, but also deception, villainy and the redeeming power of grief. It seems to have been a great favourite with Elizabethan and Jacobean audiences, and remains one with today's.

MUCH ADO ABOUT NOTHING

MESSINA, SICILY
SPAIN AND ITALY IN THE LATE THIRTEENTH CENTURY

THE ISLAND OF SICILY IS UNDER SPANISH RULE. DON PEDRO, PRINCE OF ARAGON, HAS COME TO THE ISLAND TO DEAL WITH HIS ILLEGITIMATE HALF-BROTHER, DON JOHN, WHO HAS BEEN FIGHTING ON THE SIDE OF ARAGON'S ENEMIES.

DON PEDRO HAS WON A DECISIVE BATTLE AND CAPTURED DON JOHN. HAVING FORGIVEN HIS BROTHER, DON PEDRO IS HEADING TOWARDS THE CITY OF MESSINA TO CELEBRATE HIS VICTORY.

The Kingdom of Aragon

ARAGON

Barcelona

Valencia

SARDINIA

Cagliari

ITALY

Naples

Messina

SICILY

List Of Main Characters
Dramatis Personae

VISITING MEMBERS OF THE SPANISH ARMY

COUNT CLAUDIO

An Italian nobleman of Florence

DON PEDRO

Prince of Aragon

SIGNOR BENEDICK

An Italian nobleman of Padua

DON JOHN

Illegitimate half-brother of Don Pedro

BALTHASAR

Musician to Don Pedro

BORACHIO

Servant to Don John

CONRADE

Gentleman companion of Don John

LEONATO

The governor of the city

ANTONIO

His brother

HERO

His daughter,
in love with Claudio

BEATRICE

His niece, at odds
with Benedick

URSULA

Waiting woman to Hero

MARGARET

Waiting woman to Hero,
and Borachio's lady-love

CITIZENS OF MESSINA

GEORGE SEACOAL

A member of the City Watch

HUGH OATCAKE

A member of the City Watch

A SEXTON

(Francis Seacoal)

FRIAR

(Francis)

DOGBERRY

Chief constable

VERGES

Another constable

EXTRAS

WATCHMEN
ATTENDANTS
MESSENGERS
MUSICIANS

13

14

Oh dear, he'll be all over poor Claudio like a **rash**. It sounds as if the unlucky man has a nasty case of **the Benedicks** ...

Don Pedro is here **already**!

Leonato, my friend! I am sorry to trouble you with another visit so soon.

It is **no** trouble to entertain you, Your Grace.

I believe this is your daughter, Hero.

That is what her mother told me ...

Did you fear the lady might have a **different** father?

No, Signor: for you were only a **child** at the time.

He's got you **there**, Benedick!

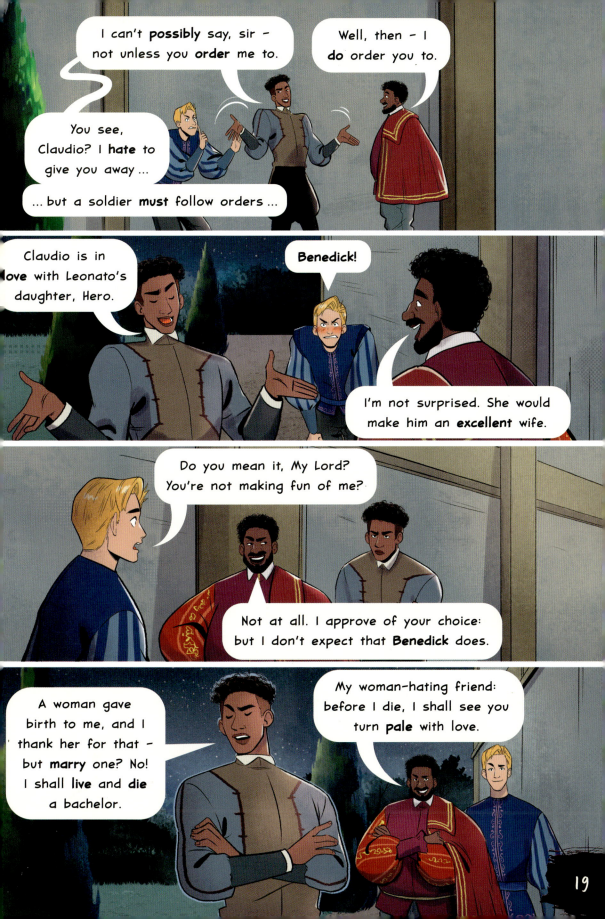

19

DON PEDRO AND CLAUDIO DON'T KNOW THAT THE SPOT THEY HAVE CHOSEN FOR A CHAT IS ALREADY OCCUPIED BY TWO TRUANT SERVANTS – ONE OF ANTONIO'S MEN, AND DON JOHN'S STOOGE, BORACHIO.

Does Leonato have a son?

No, only his daughter, Hero. Is it true that you love her?

When we called here before the battle, I **liked** her ...

... but then, my thoughts were of **war**, not **love**.

Now that we've returned, I realise how much she means to me.

Then I will speak to her father.

I'm guessing that is the favour you want from me.

It **is**, My Lord. If you only knew how much I **love** Hero ...

Spare me the details! I have an idea. After supper, Leonato plans to hold a masked ball.

When we are all in **disguise**, I shall pretend to Hero that I am **you**.

ANTONIO IS NOT SLOW TO BRING THE GOOD NEWS HE HAS HEARD TO HIS BROTHER, LEONATO.

Leonato! **Brother!** I've been looking **everywhere** for you ...

What is it, Antonio?

My man overheard the Prince and young Claudio talking in the orchard.

GASP

PANT

Don Pedro told Claudio that he loves your daughter, **Hero** ...

... and means to talk to you about it at the ball this evening.

This man of yours – is he a sharp-witted fellow?

I'll call him. Ask him **yourself** if you don't believe me.

No, no – I shall do nothing until Don Pedro speaks. But I'll tell Hero about this, so that if it happens she will be **ready** with an answer. We must go and find her ...

ACT 2

AFTER SUPPER, LEONATO AND HIS GUESTS ASSEMBLE FOR THE MASKED BALL.

I didn't see Don John at supper.

He's such a **misery**! Just **looking** at him gives me heartburn.

If you took **half** of Benedick and **half** of Don John, and mixed them together ...

... you **might** end up with a man worth looking at.

No doubt – but you will **never** get a husband, Niece, unless you learn to **guard your tongue**.

Yes, a man like that – with money in his purse – would appeal to **any** woman.

She's too quarrelsome by **half**.

28

29

But I suppose all's fair in love and war. I was a **fool** to trust Don Pedro!

Goodbye, Hero!

Oh, for goodness' sake–

SOB

CHOKE

CLAUDIO!

Eh? What?

What's the matter? You **know** the Prince has won your Hero ...

I hope they'll be very **happy** together!

Do you **really** think the Prince would deceive you like that?

Leave me alone! I'm going!

SLAM

Poor wounded bird! Now he'll creep into the long grass to hide ...

35

No, My Lord; you are too **fine** a husband for everyday use – unless I could have another one for working days ...

... forgive me; I'm talking nonsense.

I don't mind if you make fun of me. You must have been born in a happy hour.

My mother always said a star danced when I was born.

Cousins, God bless you!

There goes a **lively** lady!

It's true she is **seldom** serious, My Lord.

She doesn't seem to want a husband.

Oh, no. She sends **all** her suitors packing.

She would make an excellent wife for **Benedick**!

Ha, ha, ha! My Lord, they would drive each other **mad** in a **week**!

Claudio, what date shall we set for your wedding?

Tomorrow?

A week today, my dear son; we have a lot of preparations to make.

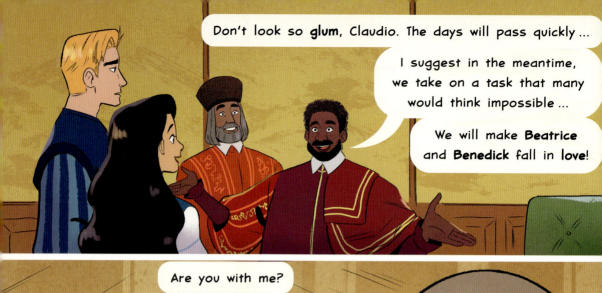

Don't look so **glum**, Claudio. The days will pass quickly ...

I suggest in the meantime, we take on a task that many would think impossible ...

We will make **Beatrice** and **Benedick** fall in **love**!

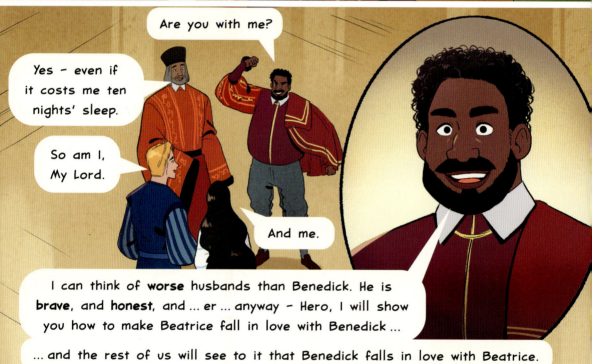

Are you with me?

Yes – even if it costs me ten nights' sleep.

So am I, My Lord.

And me.

I can think of **worse** husbands than Benedick. He is **brave**, and **honest**, and ... er ... anyway – Hero, I will show you how to make Beatrice fall in love with Benedick ...

... and the rest of us will see to it that Benedick falls in love with Beatrice.

If we succeed, Cupid can hang up his bow! We will be the **only** true love gods!

HA HA HA HA HA

They say that Count Claudio **will** marry Leonato's daughter, after all.

Yes, My Lord, but I can put a stop to it.

How?

I've told you that Margaret, Hero's lady's maid, fancies me?

I remember – but **so what?**

Go to your brother. Warn him he risks his honour by arranging for his friend Claudio to marry a woman as faithless as Hero.

And what good will **that** do?

It'll make your brother look a **fool**, drive Claudio **mad**, ruin Hero and kill Leonato. Was there anything else you wanted?

To make them pay, I'll try **anything.**

39

It **amazes** me that a man like Claudio can **scoff** at marriage one minute...

... and get **married** the next!...

Shhh... There he is...

... that a man whose **only** music was the trumpet and drum of **war**...
...will now listen **only** to the ghastly twanging of a **lute**.

TEE HEE HEE

CHUCKLE

MFFFFFF

SSSSSH!

One woman may be fair...

... another, wise ...

... a third, honest ...

... but until I find **all** those qualities in **one** woman, I shall marry **no** woman!

Come along, My Lord!

Bring your lute, Balthasar!

Oh, **no**! Don Pedro and Lover Boy! It's time I wasn't here...

41

42

43

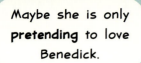

Maybe she is only **pretending** to love Benedick.

No, no, no! You only have to **look** at her to see how she is **suffering** ...

Go on – the fish is about to bite ...

Why, what does she **do**?

Why, she ... and **then** she ... Claudio, what did Hero tell you she did?

What? Oh, yes – she said (whisper, whisper, whisper ...)

Passion?! For **me**??!! **Beatrice???!!!**

You **amaze** me! Who would have thought her capable of such **mad passion**?

I'd think the others were pulling my leg, but Leonato wouldn't do that.

Has she told **Benedick** how she feels?

No, and she swears she **never** will. That's why she is so **unhappy**.

Hero says Beatrice stays awake **all night**, writing letters to him ...

... but she tears them all up in despair, crying, "He will only **laugh** at me!" If this goes on, I'm afraid she may do something desperate!

I can't think why Benedick is **acting** like this. He's a **good** man ...

... and **wise** ...

@*#$*!

... and **brave**, too.

Certainly, if he can pick a fight with anyone **weaker** than him.

Well, Leonato, I am sorry for your niece. Poor Beatrice. She's worth **ten** of Benedick.

Shall we go in to dinner, My Lord?

If he doesn't fall in love with Beatrice after **this**, I'll eat my **hat**!

SNORT

TITTER

SNIGGER

This **can't** be a trick. They were so **serious** ...

Now, if only Hero and her maid can fool Beatrice the same way ... they'll **both** think the other loves them.

We'll send Beatrice to bring Benedick in to dinner!

... and Hero and Beatrice are like **sisters**! It **must** be true! If Beatrice **loves** me - it would be ungrateful not to love her back.

46

She turns **every** man inside out, making his strengths into weaknesses.

SNIIPPP

You're right. It's **very** mean of her.

Of course it is, but if I said **anything**, she'd flay me alive with her wit! I'll tell Benedick to stay **away** from her ...

... and to make it easier for him, I'll make up some **horrid** stories to show her in a bad light.

You wouldn't tell **lies** about your own cousin!

Lady Beatrice would be **mad** to turn down a handsome, witty man like **Signor Benedick!**

He is the **best** man in Italy – apart from my **dear** Claudio, of course.

I can't hear what they're saying – I must get closer.

MEANWHILE, THE CITY WATCH, MESSINA'S POLICE FORCE, IS PREPARING FOR ANOTHER NIGHT OF PEACE-KEEPING.

Left, right, left, right, left right – form a line, men.

Men of the City Watch! If you are not good men and true, may you suffer **eternal** salvation!

'damnation'

Which of them is the most deserting ...

'deserving'

to be our deputy?

George Seacoal is, Constable Dogberry. He can read and write.

Watchman Seacoal, you are thought to be the most senseless ...

'sensible'

... man we have. Therefore you must comprehend...

'apprehend'

Why, Watchman Oatcake, you ... and then you ...

... all fragrant...

'vagrant'

... rascals. You can arrest **any** man in the Prince's name.

What if he won't be arrested?

...you tell him to be **off**, and call the rest of the Watch, and thank God you have got rid of a troublemaker!

If he won't be arrested, he is **not** a loyal subject of the Prince.

Exactly, Constable Verges, and our job is to keep the peace among the **Prince's** subjects. Everyone else will have to keep their **own** peace.

Therefore, see you don't make a lot of **noise** in the streets ...

WILL YOU SHUT UP DOWN THERE? SOME PEOPLE ARE TRYING TO SLEEP!

Ssssh! You must bear in mind that too much chatter and babble is contagious ...

'outrageous'

Ssssh! and not to be endured.

Don't worry, sir – we'd rather **sleep** than **talk**.

That's right – we know how the Watch works.

Good thinking that. When you're asleep, you can't **upset** anyone.

Just make sure nobody steals your weapons.

And at closing time, you **must** go round the alehouses and tell all the drinkers to go home to bed.

What if they won't go?

55

Those are your duties, lads. Remember that you have been given your authority by Prince Don Pedro of Aragon ...

...and you may arrest any man you suspect – even the Prince himself.

No, they can't – are you out of your mind?

According to the law, they can.

But ... but ...

... but you shouldn't arrest the Prince if he is not willing to be arrested. We of the Watch should not annoy people by arresting them.

I should think not!

Attention! Good night then, lads. If anything important happens, call me. Oh, one last thing. Signor Leonato's daughter is getting married tomorrow. Keep an eye on his house.

Yes, Constable!

All right, boys, we know what we have to do. We just sit here quietly on the church bench until two o'clock, then go home to bed.

57

58

And did they think Margaret was Hero?

Two of them did, the Prince and Claudio, but my wicked master knew she was Margaret ...

... and Claudio **swore** he would accuse Hero this morning in front of the whole congregation, and call the marriage off!

We've heard enough, lads! Let's **get** them!

We **arrest** you in the Prince's name!

Come on, you two. You have been discovered in the most **abominable** act of lechery ...

'treachery'

... that has **ever** been known in this fair city!

I **demand** a **fair** hearing!

I wouldn't bother. They must have heard everything. We're in **trouble** now!

Ursula, please go and ask my cousin **Beatrice** to come here.

Yes, My Lady.

Honestly, I think the other headpiece is better. I'm **sure** Beatrice will agree ...

Then Beatrice is a **fool**, and so are **you**. I'll wear this one.

Oh, yes – they say she looked **wonderful**!

If you say so. At least your dress suits you. I saw the dress the **Duchess of Milan** wore that everyone **raves** about ...

I **promise** you, her dress was just a **rag compared** to yours. Yours is worth **ten** of it.

Then I hope wearing it will bring me luck!

Good morning, Her–achoo!

61

HERO'S FATHER IS ALSO ON HIS WAY TO CHURCH, BUT CONSTABLE DOGBERRY HAS SOMETHING IMPORTANT TO TELL HIM...

Can I help you, Constable?

I **must** have a confidence ...

'conference'

... with you, sir ...

Can't it wait? I'm in a **hurry** ...

Well, it's like **this**, sir ...

Don't take any notice of **Constable Verges**, sir; he's an **old man**, and his wits are not what they once were ...

For goodness' **sake**, man, whatever you have to say, **get on with it!**

I beg to report, sir, that **our Watch** last night arrested a couple of the most **wicked rascals** in Messina.

Like I said, sir, my colleague is a good old man, but as they say, "There's no fool like an **old fool**".

Once he starts talking, you can't shut him up!

He's as **honest** a man as ever lived, but a bit lacking in the top storey ...

Indeed, Constable, I can see he's **no match** for you ... But I must be going ...

One word more, sir. Our Watch has **indeed** comprehended ...

'apprehended'

... two persons we wish to bring to you for **questioning**.

For **pity's sake** – question them **yourself**, and bring me their statements. I have **no time** to waste ...

My Lord, the service has **started**. You must come and give the **bride** away ...

I'm on my way!

Go, partner, and fetch Francis Seacoal, the sexton. We must subject these men to **extermination**!

'examination'

And they **MUST** be questioned **properly**, according to the **law**.

Don't worry about **that**. Just make sure we have a lawyer to write down what they say in evidence. See to it, and meet me at the jail!

65

LEONATO ARRIVES IN CHURCH IN TIME FOR THE WEDDING: BUT THAT IS THE ONLY THING THAT GOES TO PLAN...

You come here, My Lord, to marry this lady?

No.

WHISPER, WHISPER, WHISPER...

Ha ha! He comes to be married **to** her, Friar. **You** come to marry her.

Ah, yes. Ahem. If either of you know of any reason why you may **not** be married, you must declare it now.

Do **you** know any such reason, Hero?

No, My Lord.

Do **you** know any, Count?

I can answer for him – **none**!

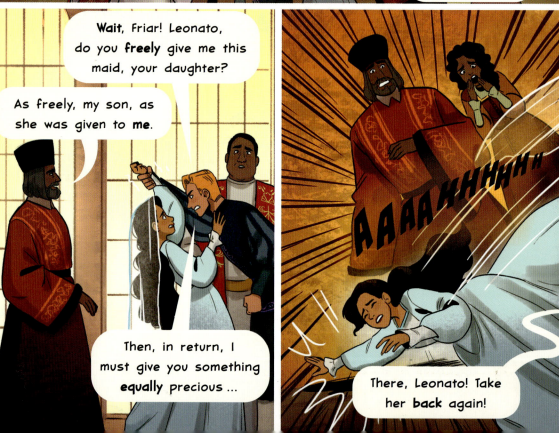

Wait, Friar! Leonato, do you **freely** give me this maid, your daughter?

As freely, my son, as she was given to **me**.

Then, in return, I must give you something **equally** precious ...

AAAAHHHHH

There, Leonato! Take her **back** again!

67

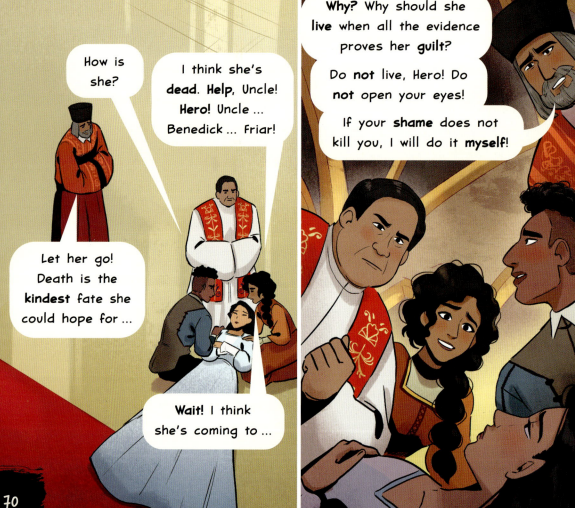

I have said nothing because I have been watching how the **lady** has dealt with these accusations.

I have seen her blush from **anger**, from **horror**, from **fear** – but from **guilt**? **No**!

Call me a **fool**. Put no trust in my **age**, my **learning** or my **experience**.

But I **tell** you, this lady is **innocent**.

Friar, that **can't** be true.

She doesn't **deny** her guilt. Why are you making **excuses** for her?

Lady, who is the man they accuse you of taking as your lover?

Ask **them**! I don't **know**.

I met **no** man, last night or any **other** night! I **swear** it!

Then the men are **deceived**.

Two of them are the very **soul** of honour ...

... but **Don John**, the Prince's **illegitimate** brother, is a lying **villain** ...

... and **Don Pedro** will **not** see him for what he is.

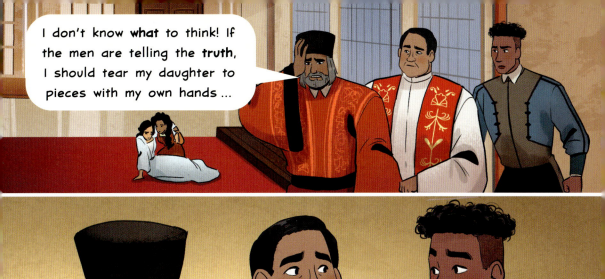

I don't know **what** to think! If the men are telling the **truth**, I should tear my daughter to pieces with my own hands ...

... but if they have accused her **wrongly**, the greatest man among them will live to **regret** it! I am not yet so old, or poor, or friendless that I cannot **revenge** myself on them!

Don't do anything **rash**. Let me advise you.

The men left your daughter here for dead. Let her **stay** here, secretly ...

... and tell everyone that she really **is** dead!

Mourn her; hold a memorial service; do **everything** a grieving parent would do for his child.

What good will **that** do?

When it is known that she died at the moment she was accused, many will **pity** her.

And is it not true that we do not value what we **have** until it is **lost** forever?

73

When Claudio hears that his accusation has **killed** Hero ...

... his **memory** of her will become more precious even than his **love** ...

... and even though he still thinks she is **guilty**, he will wish he had **never** accused her.

Signor Leonato, take the friar's advice.

The Prince and Claudio are my **dear** friends, but I **swear** I am on your side.

I will do **anything** that might end this nightmare.

Good. Dangerous diseases require **strong** medicines. Lady Hero, you must **die** to **live** again ...

Let us hope this wedding day is only postponed.

Lady Beatrice, you have been weeping ...

Yes – and I haven't finished yet!

Please don't.

Don't worry, it's not costing **you** anything. I do it **freely**.

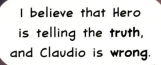

I believe that Hero is telling the **truth**, and Claudio is **wrong**.

The man who **rights** that **wrong** will earn my thanks!

Perhaps I could do that ...

Why would **you** take on such a task?

I ... **love** you. More than **anything** in the world. Isn't that **strange**?

Beatrice! You **do** love me!

Very strange. I could just as well say I loved **you** more than anything in the world – but would I **mean** it? I don't know ... I am **sorry** for my cousin.

Don't let it go to your head. You **may** change your mind later.

I won't. I **swear** that I love you.

You beat me to it. I was going to tell you that I loved **you**.

I would do **anything** for you.

All right, **prove** it ...

... KILL CLAUDIO!

75

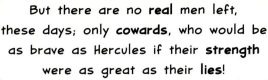

But there are no **real** men left, these days; only **cowards**, who would be as brave as Hercules if their **strength** were as great as their **lies**!

I **can't** become a man; I can only act a **woman's** part, and **die** of sorrow.

Beatrice, **wait**. I **swear** by this hand that I love you.

Then use your **hand** against my **enemies**, not to swear to empty words.

Are you absolutely **sure** that Claudio's accusations are untrue?

Yes, absolutely.

Very well. I will challenge Claudio to a duel. He will answer to **me** for his words against your cousin.

Go and comfort Hero. I must lie to Claudio and the Prince, and tell them that she is **dead**.

AARGH

ACT 5

LEONATO, NOW CONVINCED OF HERO'S INNOCENCE, IS FULL OF ANGER AGAINST HER ACCUSERS.

Leave me **alone**, Antonio. Your advice goes in one ear and out the other.

Find me someone whose grief is equal to **mine**, and I'll listen to **him**.

Brother, if you carry on like this, you will **kill** yourself.

Any mealy-mouthed **wretch** can speak comforting words about a sorrow they do not feel.

You're being **childish**.

I'm being **human**! Philosophers may claim to understand the thoughts of gods – but show me one who could ignore a toothache!

All right, but **stop** beating yourself up. Hero's accusers should take their share of the blame.

You're right.

Here come the Prince and Count Claudio. They seem in a hurry.

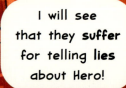

I will see that they **suffer** for telling **lies** about Hero!

You must not **say** such things, old man.

Let me **fight** him, My Lord! Never mind that he is younger and stronger than I: let **fate** decide who is right!

Leave me **alone**! I **won't** fight you!

Do you think you can get **rid** of me, just like that? You have already **killed** my daughter. If you kill **me**, too, at **least** you can boast that you've killed a **man**!

He'll have to kill **two** of us, then! Come on, you young pup. I'll show you how we fight in **Messina**!

Don't tell **me** to calm down! My beloved niece was driven to her **grave** by these villains.

Calm **down**.

Boys!

Creeps!

Maggots!

Antonio, brother ...

I **know** these two ... Lying, boastful, swaggering **light-weights**. They strut around and make **threats** – and that is **all** they dare do!

Claudio, you are a **villain**.

I challenge you to meet me **wherever** you dare, **whenever** you dare, with whatever **weapons** you choose. If you do not, you are a **coward**.

Your **lies** killed Hero, and I shall see to it that you **pay** for her death.

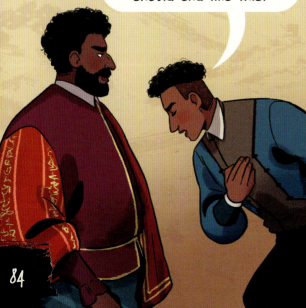

My Lord, **thank you** for your kindness to me. I am **sorry** that our friendship should end like this.

You should know that your half-brother, Don John, has **fled** from Messina.

You have, between you, killed a sweet and **innocent** lady. Farewell.

He **means** it!

I believe he **does**!

And didn't he say my **brother** had run away?

What's **this**? Two of my brother's men, **prisoners**?

I wonder what they've been up to?

Why are these men under arrest, Constable?

Sir, they have told **lies**. **Secondly**, they have spoken **untruths**.

Sixth and lastly, they have slandered a **lady**. **Thirdly**, they have given **false** evidence ...

... and to conclude, they are **lying villains**.

I'm afraid the Constable's sharp legal mind is too much for me.

Tell me in simple terms – what have you **done**?

Don Pedro, I wish to **confess**. Let Count Claudio kill me.

These men heard me tell Conrade here how your brother, Don John, **urged** me to **slander** the Lady Hero.

I told Conrade how your brother took you to the orchard ...

... where you saw **me** with **Margaret**, who wore Hero's clothes ...

... so that you **believed** you had seen **Hero** with some **lover** ...

... which caused you to **shame** her on her wedding day.

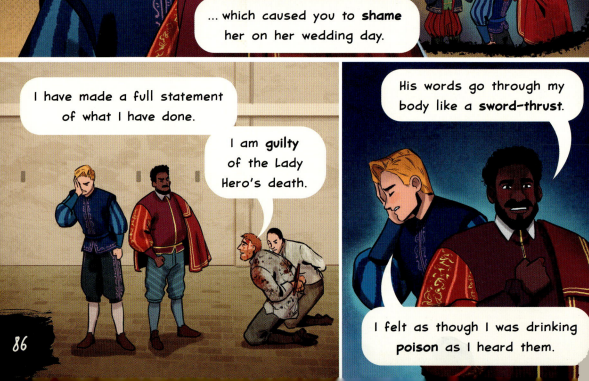

I have made a full statement of what I have done.

I am **guilty** of the Lady Hero's death.

His words go through my body like a **sword-thrust**.

I felt as though I was drinking **poison** as I heard them.

You say **my brother** put you up to this.

Yes, and paid me a **lot of** money to do it.

The sexton is telling Signor Leonato what has happened.

And I also wish to have it on record, that I am an **ass**.

Here comes Signor Leonato.

Are you the **villain** who has **killed** my poor child with your **lies**?

Yes; I, and I alone ...

That's **not** true! ...

Here stand a pair of honourable men who **share** the blame; a **third** has run away. I **thank** you, My Lords, for my daughter's death. Count it among your **brave** and **worthy** deeds.

Choose your revenge, Signor. Punish me **however** you will. But I **swear**, I was deceived.

And so was I. But I will do **anything** Signor Leonato wishes to make amends.

87

Tomorrow morning, come to my house.

You cannot be my son-in-law, but you can still be my nephew.

Nothing will bring my daughter back to life. The **most** you can do is tell the people of Messina that she was **innocent**, and pray at her **tomb** for forgiveness.

My brother Antonio has a daughter, almost **identical** to my dead child.

Marry her, as you **should have** married her cousin ...

... and I shall seek no further revenge.

My Lord, I do **not deserve** such kindness; but I accept your offer. I will do exactly as you wish.

I shall take this **wicked** man to confront Margaret.

I believe she was in league with him, **bribed** by Don John.

My Lord, I **swear** she was not. She didn't know about this plot when you saw her with me at Hero's window.

89

Didn't I tell you Hero was innocent?

So are Don Pedro and Claudio, who accused her on false evidence ...

... and Margaret, who gave them that evidence against her will.

I am glad I no longer have to fight Claudio.

Ladies, put your **veils** on.

Antonio, you **must** pretend to be Hero's father, and give her to young Claudio.

I'll **try** and do that with a straight face.

Friar, I must ask you for a favour.

To do what, Signor?

To tie the knot for me, or else tie me in knots ...

... Signor Leonato, it seems your **niece** has a mind to **marry** me; and I have set my **sights** on her ...

Sights that I, the Prince and Claudio set **for** you ...

This is the lady. I give her to you.

Then she is mine. Dear lady, let me see your face.

Not until you take her hand before the friar here, and **promise** to marry her.

Very well. Lady, I will be your husband, if you like me.

Another Hero!

One Hero died of shame. But I still **live** – and I have done **no wrong**.

How can this **be**? Hero is dead!

Lies **killed** her. Now that the lies are dead, she **lives again**.

Dear Beatrice! This good friar has agreed to **marry** us.

Oh! **Has** he, now?

What's the **matter**? Don't you **love** me?

I suppose so. Within **reason**.

Then your uncle and the Prince and Claudio were **wrong** – they said you **did**!

Don't you love **me**, then?

Oh, yes – within **reason**!

Then my cousin, Margaret and Ursula were **wrong**, too – they said **you** did!

94

Here's a miracle – our **hands** have brought us together, while our **hearts** tried to keep us apart.

And **I** will marry **you** – but only to save your life.

All right, I **will** marry you – but only out of **pity**.

So, Signor Benedick: how does it feel to be **almost** a married man?

Claudio, I seem to have been robbed of my chance of teaching you a lesson.

I've changed my mind about marriage. There's **something** to be said for it.

In your **dreams**! I just hope **Beatrice** knows what she's taking on ...

My Lord, we captured your brother as he tried to **escape** from Sicily.

Deal with him **tomorrow**, Don Pedro. I'll think of some harsh punishment for him ...

But for today – aren't we supposed to be having a **wedding** or something?

The World of Much Ado About Nothing

Where and When?

The play is set in and around the city of Messina in Sicily in the late thirteenth century. Shakespeare liked to use exotic locations and foreign-sounding names in his plays, and *Much Ado About Nothing* is partly based on an Italian novel. But the more down-to-earth characters – Dogberry, Seacoal, Oatcake, Margaret - are as British as Beefeaters and black cabs.

The Title

"Much ado" means "a lot of fuss" – so the title tells us that the play concerns people getting excited "about nothing" very important. A modern writer might have called the play, *A Storm in a Teacup*.

The Plot

The action of the play breaks down into three parts:

The events of **PART ONE** (**ACT 1** and the first part of **ACT 2**) all happen on the day Don Pedro and his officers arrive in Messina. We meet the main characters and Don Pedro offers to woo Hero on Claudio's behalf. Don John tries to cause trouble by telling Claudio that Don Pedro wants to marry Hero himself, but this ploy is only briefly successful and the marriage of Claudio and Hero is set for a week's time.

In **PART TWO** (the rest of **ACT 2** and most of **ACT 3**), Don Pedro tries to bring Beatrice and Benedick together, while Don John sets out to ruin Hero's reputation through the play-acting of Borachio and Margaret. These events take the rest of the week between the engagement of Claudio and Hero, and the arrest of Borachio and Conrade by the Watch on the eve of the wedding.

In **PART THREE**, from the wedding preparations to the end of the play, the action moves thick and fast. Dogberry and Verges stop Leonato on his way to the church, but his failure to listen to their news results in Hero being denounced and rejected by Claudio. In the rest of the play:

- Beatrice and Benedick declare their love

- Benedick challenges Claudio to a duel

- Borachio confesses to Don Pedro

- Claudio realises that he has been duped and begs forgiveness at Hero's 'tomb'

- The delayed wedding takes place; Beatrice marries Benedick, and Claudio the 'resurrected' Hero ...

The events of Part Three take place over another single day.

Sources Of Much Ado About Nothing

The plot of the *Much Ado About Nothing* is based on a story from Ludovic Ariosto's *Orlando Furioso*, an Italian epic poem translated into English in 1591, seven years before Shakespeare wrote his play. Strangely, Ariosto's tale was set in Scotland, not Italy. The virtuous Genevra is framed by a jealous suitor. The hero, Rinaldo, restores Genevra to her true love.

A more immediate source for Shakespeare's plot appeared in 1569 in a translation of a novella (short novel) by Italian author Matteo Bandello, who called his lovers Fenicia and Girondo; but Fenicia's father is called Lionato (Shakespeare's Leonato), and he serves King Piero (Don Pedro).

Although witty feuding couples had featured in earlier plays and poems, the characters of Beatrice and Benedick are entirely Shakespeare's creation.

Themes Of Much Ado About Nothing

As a comedy, the play is less focused on examining big issues than some of Shakespeare's darker work. Even so, some important ideas emerge from the fun and games.

Inner and Outer Conflict

The love of Romeo and Juliet is doomed because of the quarrel between their families. In *Much Ado About Nothing*, neither Claudio's family nor Hero's object to their getting married. The obstacle to their happiness is Don John's jealousy of his brother, who has arranged the match. Far from being grateful for Don Pedro's forgiveness, Don John is determined to spite him, and Claudio too, as Claudio was responsible for Don John's defeat and capture.

By contrast, the obstacles to Beatrice and Benedick's happiness are entirely created by themselves. It seems they have history: when Beatrice tells Don Pedro that Benedick lent his heart to her once (see page 35), she implies that they had some kind of earlier relationship that ended because she found that Benedick was "stringing her along". Now, they are so intent on scoring points off each other that for most of the play they fail to recognise what the other characters - and the audience - can clearly see: that they are in love.

Fake News

Deception and duplicity lie at the very heart of the play.

Don Pedro sets all this in motion by wooing Hero on Claudio's behalf. There is no reason for him to do this; Claudio is an adult, capable of speaking up for himself. As in his later scheme to bring Beatrice and Benedick together, Don Pedro is interfering because he likes to act the part of a benevolent father-figure.

But Don John seizes on his half-brother's idea for his own twisted ends. First he tries to convince Claudio that Don Pedro wants Hero for himself, causing Claudio to throw a massive sulk.

When this is cleared up, Don John seizes on Borachio and Margaret's imitation of Claudio and Hero to ruin Claudio's romance. In the meantime, Don Pedro, with the best of intentions, fools Beatrice and Benedick into believing that each is loved by the other.

All this plotting, and its near-disastrous consequences, occurs because not one of the characters in the play bothers to check the truth of anything they hear or see. The modern spread of 'fake news' – unfounded statements that people become convinced are true – is just a modern version of the way that otherwise sensible characters allow themselves to be deceived in the play.

Fake news works for two main reasons: people believe it because they want it to be true, or because they are afraid that it may be true. Beatrice and Benedick believe the news that each is in love with the other because they secretly want this to be true. Claudio believes that Hero is unfaithful to him because this is what he most fears.

Infidelity

Shakespeare's original script is full of rude jokes that his audience likely found hilarious, but that for a modern audience are both hard to understand and unfunny. Many of these centre on the idea of husbands and wives being unfaithful to their marriage partners.

In Shakespeare's day, a woman was seen as her husband's property. Therefore, if she was unfaithful, her husband was at fault. He would be mocked as a "cuckold", and depicted as having horns growing from his head. The word has the same root as "cuckoo", a bird that lays its eggs in other birds' nests.

When Leonato tells Don Pedro that Hero is his daughter (see page 15), he adds, "That is what her mother told me". "Did you fear the lady might have a different father?" Bendick asks, and Leonato replies, "No, Signor: for you were only a child at the time". The implication is that the grown-up Benedick is the sort of man who might have an affair with another man's wife. The exchange angers Beatrice: "Are you still talking, Signor Benedick? I can't imagine why; nobody is listening".

But the jokes about infidelity keep coming in a male slap-on-the-back-all-boys-together way for the rest of the play, even after Hero appears to have died of grief at being accused of this very fault.

Male and Female Roles

The roles of men and women in Elizabethan England are exaggerated in the play because many of the male characters are soldiers, bound by masculine codes of honour and companionship. Beatrice, the most intelligent of the female characters, uses her sharp tongue to challenge this male smugness; but she can do nothing about Claudio's accusation of Hero because she is a woman. She cannot challenge Claudio to a duel, so she must persuade Benedick to take action on her behalf. Her frustration provides one of the most highly-charged emotional moments in the play (see page 76):

> [Claudio] has scorned and slandered my cousin!
> Oh, if only I were a man! He led her to the altar, not to take her
> hand, but to dishonour her! Oh, if only I were a man!
> I would eat Claudio's heart in the marketplace!

Shakespeare's Language

Inventions

Shakespeare used more than 20,000 different words in his plays and poems. Around 1,700 of these were new or were the first recorded use of the word! He invented new words and phrases by making them up or by putting two words together to make a new one, or adding or subtracting parts of words.

Malapropisms and Dogberryisms

In Richard Brinsley Sheridan's *The Rivals*, a play written almost 200 years after *Much Ado About Nothing*, a character called Mrs Malaprop says, "She's as headstrong as an allegory on the banks of the Nile". Of course, she means "alligator".

When a character tries to use an impressive-sounding word and gets it wrong, this is called a "Malapropism".

In *Much Ado About Nothing*, Dogberry does this all the time, and has to be corrected by Verges, so much so that "Dogberryism" is another word for "Malapropism".

Prose and Poetry

Shakespeare's works were often written in a mixture of verse and prose (normal speech). Important and high-ranking characters (kings, lords, etc.) usually speak in verse. Prose is more likely to be spoken by servants.

There are 2,485 lines in *Much Ado About Nothing*. 70 per cent of these lines are in prose. In all Shakespeare's plays, only *The Merry Wives of Windsor* has a higher proportion of prose to verse.

Acts 1, 2 and 3 are mostly in prose, but in Acts 4 and 5, when tragedy threatens, most of the characters speak in 'blank verse'.

Blank Verse

This is a type of poetry that follows these rules:

- Each line has 10 or 11 syllables.
- Each line has five strong beats.

Think of a heart beating: de **DUM** de **DUM** de **DUM** de **DUM** de **DUM**. This is similar to how the beat or stress falls on the syllables in blank verse. See how this works in the line below, when Claudio accuses Hero; Leonato, unable to believe his ears, says:

De - **Dum** - de - **Dum** - de - **Dum** - de - **Dum** - de - **Dum**

Are - **these** - things - **spo** - ken - **or** - do - **I** - but - dream?

(Act 4 Scene 1)

A Soliloquy

This is a speech spoken by one character; we're listening to their thoughts. They are thinking out loud to themselves, or speaking directly to the audience, not to another character. (In the graphic novel, we have put some of these in "thought bubbles".)

An example of this is on pages 46–47, when Benedick is thinking about what he has overheard.

Sonnets

In contrast to blank verse, a sonnet is poem that has 14 lines and a strict rhyming pattern. Shakespeare was famous for his sonnets (he wrote over 150 of them).

Beatrice and Benedick write sonnets to each other in the final scene. We don't get to hear or read them, but it seems that both are pleased with the other's effort.

Fun Facts

Dogberry and Borachio

The chief constable of Messina, Dogberry, gets his name from the fruits of the dogwood bush. Its red berries look tasty but are actually bitter, as Dogberry's authority as constable is illusory.

Borachio's name comes from the Spanish word for a drunk – borachho – which is also the name for a leather wine-bottle.

Ghost Characters

In the earliest quarto version of the play, Leonato has a wife, "Innogen", who enters with him at the start of the play but who has nothing to do or say. Claudio apparently has an uncle in Messina who never appears. These are called "ghost characters" – characters that Shakespeare creates and then, finding he has no use for them, discards.

Carnival of the Animals

Many of the characters in the play are compared to animals. Claudio is a "lamb" who in battle turns into a "lion". Beatrice and Benedick are "two bears", and Benedick is also compared to a "savage bull". Dogberry, obviously, is an "ass".

Much Ado About Movies and More

1. *Béatrice et Bénédict* is the most famous opera based on the play. It was written by French composer Hector Berlioz in 1862.

2. In the 2015 Royal Shakespeare Company's stage version, recorded for broadcast, the play is called *Love's Labour's Won* because it is presented as a sequel to Shakespeare's play *Love's Labour's Lost*.

3. Indian cinema has produced two versions of the play: *Monsoon Wedding* (2001), set in modern India, and *Dil Chahata Hai* (also 2001) set in Mumbai, India and Sidney, Australia.

4. Kenneth Branagh's 1993 film starring himself as Benedick was a box-office success.

5. In 2012, Joss Whedon, whose credits include the first Avengers movie and Marvel TV show *Agents of S.H.I.E.L.D.*, made a stylish black-and-white film set in present-day Santa Monica, California, and featuring smartphones, limousines, and surveillance cameras feeding into a security centre run by Dogberry and the Watch.

Publication

Shakespeare's plays weren't printed or even written up as complete plays before they were first performed. Each actor was given his part on a scroll. They had to learn their lines from this.

The "platt" or plot of the play was a list of the scenes with the exits and entrances. This was posted backstage for the actors to follow.

Much Ado About Nothing first appeared in a quarto version in 1600.

It was republished as part of the *First Folio* in 1623, when 36 of Shakespeare's plays were published together for the first time.

Book Fact

There were three main sizes of books in Shakespeare's time.

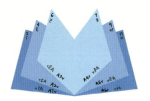

Folio

A book made from sheets of paper that are folded once to make four pages from one sheet.

Quarto

A smaller book. The sheets of paper are folded twice to make eight pages from one sheet.

Octavo

An even smaller book! The sheets of paper are folded four times to make 16 pages from one sheet.

Performing The Play!

In Shakespeare's time, drama performance and theatre spaces were developing in various ways across the globe. England was no exception.

When Shakespeare began his acting career, there were very few theatres in London.

Plays were performed in inn yards and in the halls and houses of the monarch or the wealthy. But, by the end of Shakespeare's life, plays were being performed in purpose-built theatres across London, where performances took place every day (except Sundays), all year round.

The first purpose-built London playhouse appeared in 1576 when James Burbage, father of Shakespeare's friend, Richard Burbage, constructed a building for performing plays. He called it The Theatre! The success of this space led to other playhouses being built across London.

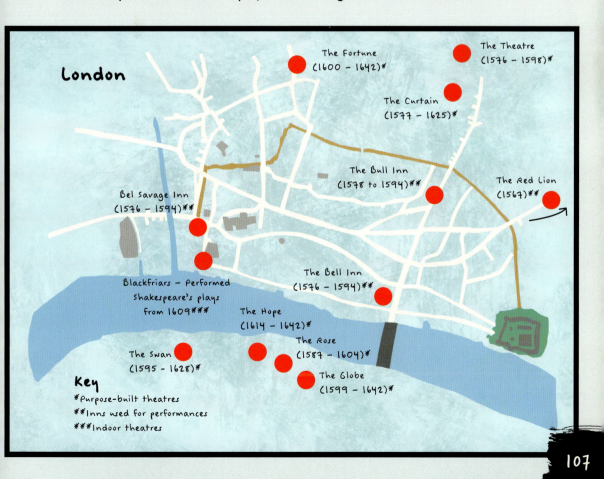

London

The Fortune
(1600 – 1642)*

The Theatre
(1576 – 1598)*

The Curtain
(1577 – 1625)*

The Bull Inn
(1578 to 1594)**

The Red Lion
(1567)**

Bel Savage Inn
(1576 – 1594)**

The Bell Inn
(1576 – 1594)**

Blackfriars – performed
shakespeare's plays
from 1609***

The Hope
(1614 – 1642)*

The Rose
(1587 – 1604)*

The Swan
(1595 – 1628)*

The Globe
(1599 – 1642)*

Key
*Purpose-built theatres
**Inns used for performances
***Indoor theatres

The Theatre

A trip to the theatre to see a play in Shakespeare's time was very different from today. People didn't sit still. They stood, walked around, shouted and chatted to each other. The audience could buy ale, wine, pies, fruit, tobacco and nuts, all while the play was being performed. The audience got as close to the action as possible, so they could hear the actors – there were no microphones in Shakespeare's day!

The plays were aimed at all levels of society – from Lords and Ladies of the court down to tradespeople and commoners. Criminals also visited the playhouses, ready to pick the pockets of unsuspecting members of the audience.

Depending on how rich (and important) you were, you could choose where to sit.

In 1594, a worker's pay was about 8 pence a day, so it meant that plays were affordable to a lot of London's population and therefore many people went to the theatre. The large theatres, such as The Globe, could hold up to 3,000 spectators, including 1,000 groundlings (see opposite).

For indoor playhouses, it was more expensive and therefore the audience members were wealthier.

The Globe Theatre was built in 1599.

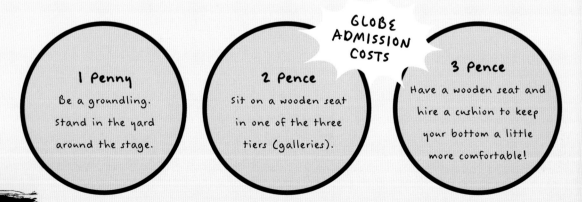

GLOBE ADMISSION COSTS

1 Penny
Be a groundling. Stand in the yard around the stage.

2 Pence
Sit on a wooden seat in one of the three tiers (galleries).

3 Pence
Have a wooden seat and hire a cushion to keep your bottom a little more comfortable!

The Globe Theatre

Open-air Playhouse

There would be a different show every afternoon. Coloured flags were used to advertise what play was being put on that day.

Red – History
Black – Tragedy
White – Comedy

Galleries

Thatched roof

Standing area groundlings

Stage
(Under stage and above stage used for special effects, storing costumes and changing rooms for actors)

6 Pence
Sit in the Lord's Gallery – rooms on either side of the balcony at the back of the stage.

12 Pence
(1 shilling)
Sit on the stage.

30 Pence
(2 shillings & 6 pence – or half a crown)
you could sit in a private box.

Glossary

The World of Shakespeare's Words

Early Modern English Language was only about 100 years old when Shakespeare started writing in the sixteenth century. Because he often wrote in verse, in order to fit the words into the necessary rhythm, some of the sentence order seems odd to us today.

As Shakespeare was writing over 400 years ago, some of the words and phrases he uses can look a bit strange. Some are so old, that we don't use them any more!

Thou, thee, thy and thine

Shakespeare uses these words A LOT. But they aren't as confusing as they seem!

thou	means	you
thee	means	you
thy	means	your
thine	means	your

Sometimes two words are put together. Watch out for the apostrophe!

'twas	means	it was
'twere	means	it were
'tis	means	it is
is't	means	is it

Sometimes words have extra letters. Take off the t or st and see what's left!

hast	means	has
wilt	means	will
dost	means	does
thinkst	means	think
hath	means	has
didst	means	did

Some more old words:

art	means	are
ere	means	before
forfeit	means	penalty
forsaken	means	abandoned
hence	means	from here
hie	means	go (hurry)
wherefore	means	why
ye	means	you
yonder	means	there
fie!	means	an exclamation of disapproval

Shakespeare Timeline

We often have no clear information about the dates of Shakespeare's plays. Scholars who study Shakespeare have to rely on information such as the way each play is put together, the language Shakespeare uses and details in the text that connect to parts of history.

Therefore, the dates of the plays given below are 'best guesses' as to the years in which they were written and first performed.

1558	Queen Mary I dies and her sister, Queen Elizabeth I, takes the throne of England.
1564	Shakespeare is born. Horse-drawn coaches first appear in England.
1567	The first purpose-built theatre in England is built – The Red Lion in Stepney, London.
1576	The Theatre is built in London by James Burbage. 180,000 people now live in London. 300,000 live in Paris, France.
1582	Shakespeare marries Anne Hathaway.
1582	The theatres close down in London due to an outbreak of plague. Thousands of people die. London's first waterworks is founded.
1583	Susanna (Shakespeare's daughter) is born. (See also 1585)
1584	Ivan The Terrible, first ruler of Russia, dies.
1585	Hamnet and Judith (twins – Shakespeare's son and daughter) are born.
1587	Shakespeare leaves Stratford-upon-Avon and his family for London. The Rose Theatre is built in London by Philip Henslowe (on Bankside). Mary Queen of Scots is executed.
1588	The Spanish Armada invade England, but are defeated.
1590/1	Shakespeare's first plays, **THE TWO GENTLEMAN OF VERONA** and **THE TAMING OF THE SHREW,** are performed.
1591	Shakespeare dedicates his poem, *Venus and Adonis,* to the Earl of Southampton. This poem earns him a lot of money! Tea is first drunk in England.
1592	Shakespeare is mentioned in the press as an up-and-coming playwright. Plague! All London playhouses are closed for two years. Many of the acting companies tour the country. Shakespeare begins writing poems. The Imjin Wars between Japan and Korea begin.
1593	Playwright and friend of Shakespeare, Christopher Marlowe, is killed in a brawl.
1594	Shakespeare's poem, *The Rape of Lucrece,* is published. Again, it is dedicated to the Earl of Southampton.
1595	Shakespeare becomes a shareholder in The Lord Chamberlain's Men (a very successful and popular acting company). **ROMEO AND JULIET**

1596	Shakespeare's son, Hamnet, dies. Shakespeare's father, John, is granted a coat of arms.
	England sees its first tomatoes – and its first flushing toilet.
	A MIDSUMMER NIGHT'S DREAM
1597	Shakespeare buys New Place in Stratford – one of the largest houses in the town.
	Transportation to English colonies is first used as a punishment for criminals.
1598	**MUCH ADO ABOUT NOTHING**
1599	The Globe Theatre is built.
1601	**HAMLET**
	Shakespeare's father dies.
1603	Queen Elizabeth dies.
	James VI of Scotland takes the throne with the title James I.
	Plague hits London. Over 30,000 people die. The theatres are closed again.
	The Lord Chamberlain's Men change their name to The King's Men.
	They perform at the King's courts and are recognised as the leading theatre company of the time.
1604	The Globe reopens.
1605	The Gunpowder Plot fails to blow up King James and his ministers.
	In Spain, Cervantes publishes Part 1 of the world's first novel, *Don Quixote*.
1606	**MACBETH**
	Theatres are ordered to close if the weekly number of people who die from the plague rises above 30.
	Theatres closed July – December.
1607	Shakespeare's daughter Susanna marries John Hall, a physician in Stratford.

	Shakespeare's brother, Edmund (an actor), dies.
	Founding of Jamestown, Virginia – first English colony in North America.
1608	Shakespeare's mother, Mary, dies.
	Shakespeare becomes a grandfather! Elizabeth is born to Susanna and John Hall.
	The King's Men begin to perform at an indoor theatre at Blackfriars.
	The telescope is invented by a Dutch scientist and used by Galileo.
1609	Shakespeare's *Sonnets* are published.
	The Blue Mosque is built in Constantinople (now Istanbul).
1610	Shakespeare spends more time in Stratford.
1611	**THE TEMPEST**
1612	Shakespeare's brother, Gilbert, dies.
	The decimal point is first used by German mathematician Pitiscus.
	The Dutch establish a trading post on Manhattan Island (later New York).
1613	The Globe Theatre burns down during a performance of Henry VIII.
	Shakespeare buys a house in Blackfriars, London.
1614	The Globe Theatre is rebuilt.
1616	Shakespeare's daughter, Judith, marries Thomas Quiney, a Stratford wine merchant.
	Shakespeare dies.
1623	Shakespeare's plays are published. the *First Folio* contains 36 of his plays.